Storyline Scotland

Book 3 by Moira Miller

Oliver & Boyd

...ultant for the series, Glenys M. Smith

...ledgments

We are grateful to the following for supplying photographs and information and giving permission for their use: Aerofilms Limited, p. 32; BBC Hulton Picture Library, pp. 36, 128; Glasgow Museum of Transport, pp. 56, 57; National Galleries of Scotland, pp. 60 (centre), 64, 65, 88, 97 (foot); National Portrait Gallery, 97 (top two); Raymond Mander & Joe Mitchenson Theatre Collection, p. 72; Scottish Development Department (Crown Copyright), pp. 13, 16, 17, 85, 96; Scottish Television PLC, cover; Scottish Tourist Board, pp. 4, 20, 49, 60 (top & foot), 112; 202 Squadron (Search and Rescue) RAF Lossiemouth, p. 23; Topham, pp. 9, 51, 122.

Illustrated by Leonora Box, Jon Davis, George Fryer, Nicholas Hewetson, Annabel Large, John Marshall, Rob Norman, Mark Peppé.

Oliver & Boyd
Robert Stevenson House
1–3 Baxter's Place
Leith Walk
Edinburgh EH1 3BB

A Division of Longman Group Ltd

ISBN 0 05 003564 9

First published 1985

© Moira Miller 1985

Set in 12/18pt Monophoto Plantin

Produced by **Longman Group (FE) Ltd**
Printed in Hong Kong

Contents

Through the Crinan Canal

My name is Anne. When we went back to school
again this year, the teacher asked us all where we had
spent our summer holidays. I said we had gone on
my Uncle Leslie's boat, and he had taken us through
the Crinan Canal. The teacher said that the canal was
a real piece of history. You see it was built about
1820 by a very famous engineer called Thomas
Telford.

   He didn't really build it all. There was an old canal
there before, but Thomas Telford improved it. He
made it very much easier for ships to sail from places
like Glasgow up the west coast of Scotland.

The teacher showed us on a map how there is
a long strip of land called Kintyre and the canal cuts
across the top from Ardrishaig to Crinan, where it is
narrow. The ships don't have to go all the way down
one side and up the other again and it saves them a
lot of time. I was asked to stand up and tell the class
all about it, and they all said it was very interesting.
I wonder what they would have said if I had told them
about my Uncle Leslie and what really happened.

You see my Uncle Leslie is a bit funny. Sometimes
he's the kind of funny that makes you laugh – and
sometimes he's not! He sent us a postcard to say that
the boat was at Ardrishaig and that he was going to

take it through the canal. You need at least three people to go through the canal with a boat. He thought Mum and Dad could help, and John and I would enjoy ourselves. I don't know why he thought that, because Mum always gets seasick on boats. She can't even row across the pond in the park. The only thing John ever wants to do is play football, and Dad was supposed to be painting the bedroom that weekend. Mum said he only went so that he didn't have to do the painting. I think he would have been better to have stayed at home and painted after all.

We left very early in the morning from Glasgow. Mum filled up the car with jerseys and wellington boots and anoraks and socks. She said it was in case we got wet. Dad said she was daft and the weather was beautiful. It was very sunny and I thought he was right.

When we got to Ardrishaig it was still warm, but there were some clouds in the sky. We met Uncle Leslie at the harbour and he said we looked as if we had come ready for an ocean voyage. But Mum insisted on us taking all the jerseys and boots and other things on to the boat.

There were quite a few boats tied up in the harbour and we had to climb over two others to get to Uncle Leslie's. It took quite a long time back and forward with all the clothes, so Uncle Leslie told John to stand on the deck and he would throw the things across to him. It worked quite well until it came to my wellingtons, and John missed one. It flew right over his head and landed in the canal. Before John could catch it, it turned over, filled up with water and sank. Mum was not too happy about that. I was quite pleased. I hate wellingtons anyway, and one is no use on its own.

Once we had everything on the boat, Uncle Leslie asked Dad to untie the ropes while he started the engine. To get from the harbour into the canal you have to go through the road bridge. It lifts up, like a castle drawbridge, and all the traffic has to wait while the boats go through. When the bridge went up there was a bus on one side, and a motorbike on the other.

Uncle Leslie put on his captain's hat, and went up on deck to start the engine. "Right, we're off!" he shouted.

But nothing happened. It was really awful. He kept trying, again and again. The people in the bus were getting more and more annoyed, so were all the other cars behind them. There were about six of them now. The motorbike man shouted something, but Mum said just to ignore him. I went down into the cabin where they couldn't see me.

It was a long time before the engine started, but at last it coughed. Smoke came out of the pipe at the back of the boat, and we moved slowly forward into the first lock. If you've never been in a lock before I suppose it is quite frightening the first time. When you go in, the water is at the bottom. The canal is very narrow in a lock. There are high stone walls on either side of you, green and slippery with weeds. In front of you there are two huge high wooden gates that hold back the water in the canal. There are two gates behind you as well, which are closed tightly. Someone has to open a little flap, called a sluice, in the front gates and slowly let water into the lock so that it fills up. When the water in the lock is level with the water in the canal in front of you, you open the front gates and float out.

It sounds easy, doesn't it? The only trouble was that Dad was on the boat with us. He should have been on the bank to close the gates, tie up the boat while it was in the lock, and open the sluice. Uncle Leslie started muttering things at him, so Dad climbed up the lock gate to get out. I really didn't think he could do it. It's quite surprising sometimes what your parents can do.

When Dad opened the sluice the water rushed in very fast. The boat tossed around a lot. John and

Mum held tight to the ropes that tied us up to the
bank and we floated slowly up to the top. Dad
opened the front gate, and there we were, sailing off
into the canal. The engine started first time, because
there was nobody watching us. Dad closed the lock
gates, ready for the next boat going down, and
jumped on to the deck.

We went through quite a few locks. At some of them Dad had to get out and open the gates himself. At others there were people walking on the path who stopped to help him. They all seemed to enjoy watching the boat going through. At some of the locks there's a cottage where the lock-keeper lives. He comes out to help you through and operates the gates for you. We were really doing quite well. Uncle Leslie was saying what fun it all was, when the engine broke down again. It was a pity, because even Mum had smiled a little bit by that time.

Dad and Uncle Leslie took the cover off the engine and started to take it to pieces. John tried to help, but he only got in the way. Mum went inside the cabin to make a cup of tea and I lay on the deck in the sun. Not for long though. It suddenly went very dark and a wet blob fell on my face. It was pouring before I got inside the boat. The rain sounds funny in a boat. From the inside you can hear it pattering on the roof of the cabin, like being underneath an umbrella. If you put your head outside you can hear it falling in the water. It makes a soft hissing sound. Dad and Uncle Leslie got more and more bad-tempered with the engine, but they managed to mend it at last.

We got under way again. That's what Uncle Leslie said you called it when the boat was moving. There were more locks, and a hotel where people were sitting in a dining room eating and watching us out in the rain. Mum would have liked to stop there. But Dad and Uncle Leslie were so filthy and wet, I don't think they would have let us in.

At one lock the keeper told us we wouldn't be able to go right through to Crinan, because it was Saturday. Uncle Leslie asked what was special about Saturdays. The keeper said that the road bridge that crossed the canal at Bellanoch closed early, and stayed closed all day on Sunday. We were going to have to wait at Bellanoch until Monday morning.

Uncle Leslie and Dad were annoyed, but I think Mum was quite pleased really. When we got to Bellanoch we tied the boat up beside the bridge. It was nearly tea-time and the rain had stopped, so John and I had a game of football on the bank with some children who lived in the house across the road. Mum made bacon and eggs and tea with bread and butter. Dad and Uncle Leslie had a wash and I think everyone felt much better afterwards.

Sunday was very quiet. The sun shone all day and we climbed up the hill behind the houses. We could see away back along the canal from the top. In front of us was the harbour at Crinan. The sea was very blue and away in the distance were the islands where Uncle Leslie was taking the boat. It was really beautiful, in fact it was an amazing day. Nothing went wrong and nobody had an argument with anybody. Even John was quite nice, which makes a change for him.

On Monday we took the boat down through the last locks and out into the sea. While no one was looking John and I dropped my other wellington boot over the side into the harbour. It floated for a bit on the surface, and then turned over and sank. John said it was a giant step for mankind; I had one foot at each end of the Crinan Canal! Mum said we were daft when she found out, but she wasn't too angry. I think she was just quite pleased that we were going to catch a bus back to Ardrishaig to collect the car.

I wonder if Thomas Telford ever dropped his boots in the canal?

The Black House

What sort of house do you live in? Does it look like this?

Have you ever stopped to wonder why the roof is the shape it is, or why the windows are the size they are? What is your house made of? Is there a reason for building it where it is?

Houses are very important to us. In the beginning people used to live in caves. Groups of families would live together in one place. Then men would go out from the cave to hunt and fish and find food for the women and children. Gradually people realised that if they built their own caves, or houses, they could live nearer to a river or the sea where they fished. They could also live on ground suitable for growing crops.

Some people liked to be able to move around, so they built houses that could move with them. The Indians of North America made tents, called teepees, from poles and skins. They were able to move their villages across the prairies, following the herds of buffalo which they killed for meat and skins. In the far north, the Eskimo people used the only building material they had. Snow! They used blocks of snow to build round houses, called igloos, to protect themselves from the weather. In hot countries like Africa, people built houses of mud bricks. The walls were thick to protect them from the heat, and the tiny windows let in only a little of the glaring sunlight.

It seems strange that in the north of Scotland, on the cold windswept islands of the Hebrides, the Scots also built houses with thick walls and tiny windows. But they were built like that for a quite different reason. The thick walls kept the cold out, and the tiny windows helped to keep the heat in.

Winter in the islands has always been harsh. At first people built round beehive-shaped shelters, in which they all lived together. These shelters were also used as forts to protect them from their enemies. Later, when peace came, families left to live on their own, and gradually the houses changed to suit their needs. They were no longer high and round, to be used as look-out towers. They were built long and low so that the winter gales would pass over them. The materials used were the stones and turf that made up the land of the islands. These buildings became known as black houses and for many years they were the only homes known to the island people.

Come and look at one with us. The first thing you will notice is that the walls of the house are not very high. Built of the local grey stones piled on top of one another, the walls are lower than a man's head. Around the top is a mat of grass, and above that the roof. It is not a slate roof, or even one made of straw thatch, but a thick mat of turf cut from the hillside around the house. It is held down firmly all round by ropes tied to heavy stones. One thing is missing – there is no chimney. Come inside and you will see why.

When we open the door to step inside, we can see how thick the wall is. If you stand in the doorway and stretch your arms out as far as they will go, the distance between the outside wall of the house and the inside one is much further than you can reach. This is because there are really two walls, one built inside the other. The island people did not have cement, so the stones were piled one on top of another, leaving gaps between them. In winter the wind would have blown through these gaps making the house very cold inside. So another wall was built inside the first, and the space between the two was filled with sand or earth. It makes the little house very warm in the winter.

Come in and close the door. It is very dark inside. The windows are small to keep out the cold, and they also keep out the light. You must stand still for a moment until your eyes become used to the dark, and then you can see. Perhaps this is why it was called a black house!

Black house, Arnol, Isle of Lewis – the kitchen hearth and peat fire.

The wooden beams supporting the turf roof can clearly be seen in this part of the house, where animals were kept in the winter.

The floor beneath our feet is made of earth. It has been trampled flat and smooth by the many people who have lived in the house. In the middle of the room a small bright fire burns on some flat stones. There is no fireplace or chimney. The smoke drifts up into the darkness of the roof above our heads and some of it escapes through a hole. Look up and you will see how the roof is supported on a spider's web of wooden beams.

The ends of the beams rest on the inside walls of the house, and they are tied together at the top. Lying across them, running the length of the house, is one long beam. This is the rooftree. It is probably the most valuable thing in the whole house. There are not many trees on the islands and if you could find a strong length of timber to support your whole roof, then you were very lucky indeed. Many islanders removed the rooftree when they moved house and took it with them. Families building a new house used to search the beaches for driftwood. They might find the keel of an old wooden fishing boat. That made a perfect rooftree.

The few pieces of furniture in the house are very simple. Sit by the fire on a little wooden stool and look around you.

Over by the wall there is a dresser. This is a cupboard with open shelves above it, where the family would keep their dishes and food. There is an old table, and several large wooden chests where clothes were kept. Behind you there is a piece of furniture that looks like a very large cupboard with two doors. It reaches from the floor almost to the roof, making this part of the house into two separate rooms. Open the doors and look inside.

Instead of shelves or drawers you will find it is a bed, covered with a patchwork quilt. Climb in and close the doors behind you. On a summer night it must have been dark and stuffy, but it would be very cosy on a cold winter night. It was not very comfortable though, as the mattress was probably stuffed with straw, and the blankets would be made of rough woollen cloth. If you climb out and look round the back of the bed you will find another little room with another box bed, and perhaps a chest or stool.

Above your head is the same turf roof and all around the smell of the smoke from the fire on the hearth stones. Also under the same roof, on the other side of the fire from the bed, there is a high wooden wall. Let us look behind that.

There is straw, a wooden trough and stalls where animals can be penned in. It seems strange to us to keep animals other than small pets in the house, but in the winter this is what the people of the islands did. They brought their few cows or goats in under the same roof. This kept the animals safe and warm, and the animals in turn spread their heat through the house. The family must have longed for the warmer spring weather when they could be taken back out to the fields again, and the pens could be cleaned out!

It must have been a hard life living in a black house like this. It would have been noisy, dirty, and very smelly, with the smoke from the fire everywhere. But these houses, like the Indian teepee or the Eskimo igloo, were part of the lives of the people. They could be built very easily and very quickly. It was said that if a whole village helped they could build a house and have it completed and ready for the family in one day.

Black houses stood for hundreds of years, stout and strong against the storms of winter. Many generations of island families grew up in them, and there are children today whose great-grandparents were probably born in a black house just like this one.

Today the island people live in houses with large doors and bright sunny windows. They look like homes anywhere. They are sunny and comfortable. I wonder, though, if they sometimes sit by the fire on a winter evening complaining about the draughts that blow in under the door, and think of the warm thick walls that the wind could never blow through.

Modern Lewis home with the old black house beside it.

Helicopter Rescue

It was the third holiday Andrew had spent in the village. You might have thought he would have wanted to go somewhere else, just for a change, but the village was the best place he knew.

The holiday house stood on the headland overlooking the beach. As soon as the car was unpacked, Andrew ran out to see what was the same as last year, and what was different.

The old tree at the bottom of the garden had been blown down at last by the winter gales, and the rusty gate had been painted bright orange. But the garden seat still had three bricks holding up one corner and the bay below the house with the harbour and the fishing boats was still the same.

Andrew closed his eyes and listened. The sounds were all the same too. Over by the harbour he could hear the steady thunk-thunk-thunk of a boat engine, and the greedy screaming gulls which sat on the roof of the fish shed, looking for food. He could hear the quiet swish of the waves on the rocks below the house. And behind everything, if you listened very carefully, there was a deep roar. That was the best sound of all. Andrew turned away from the sea and the sound grew louder. It came from the airfield on the other side of the headland. Just as Andrew's Mum came out of the house the roar changed to a high-pitched whine.

"He's taking off!" yelled Andrew.

They stood, deafened by the noise as the dark green fighter plane screamed low over the house, rattling the windows.

"Great!" whispered Andrew, watching the orange glow of the jet engine vanishing out to sea.

"I came to tell you tea's ready," yelled Mum, above the noise.

"But there might be a helicopter," Andrew shouted back. "Can't I have a sandwich out here?"

"You've got two weeks yet!" said Mum. "Come on in."

Andrew was up early next morning. He knew that the rescue helicopter would come over just after breakfast. It happened every morning. They either dropped a man in the sea and practised lifting him out, or put him down on the cliffs and lifted him from there. This morning it was the sea. The big yellow Sea King whirled out over the house and hovered over the bay. As Andrew watched, one member of the crew was lowered down into the water on a rope. He wore an orange waterproof suit and a life jacket. Andrew could see him wave to the pilot.

Air-sea rescue practice from a Sea King helicopter.

The rope went back up and another man came down to pick him up.

For the next half hour Andrew sat and watched as they practised dropping and picking up the man in the water. At last they picked him up for the final time and swept back across the house to the airfield. Andrew waved as they went over.

"They're very good," said Dad. He had come out to watch the last ten minutes.

"Better than the fighters," said Andrew. "There's more to see. I'd love to go up in one."

"There's no chance of that," said Dad. "They're far too busy, these boys!"

The holiday flew past, and Andrew had a great time. He swam every day, went out in a fishing boat, watched the planes and helicopters, and played with the boys from the village. There was one boy called Dave who was a special friend.

Dave knew all the best places to play. He showed Andrew where there were caves round the cliffs. He took him up over the fields to the fence round the airfield, where they could sit and watch the control tower and the runway. One day Dave borrowed his Dad's radio and they fiddled with the knobs until they could hear the man in the tower talking to the planes. The voices crackled back and forward as the small green fighter planes screamed over their heads. They flew so low they could see the pilots inside quite clearly, and the noise seemed to shake the ground under their feet.

"Come on," said Dave after a while, "I'll show you another cave. This is the best one, it's difficult to climb up, so nobody else goes there."

He jumped up and ran across the field to the path that led to the cliffs. Andrew looked back to watch another fighter screech to a halt on the runway and then followed him. Dave led the way down to the beach at the bottom of the cliffs. Andrew ran behind him round the slippery seaweed-covered stones.

"Does the tide come up here?" he shouted.

"Not for hours," said Dave. "We'll be back before then." He scrambled up the rocks and started to climb the cliff face.

"I don't like this," said Andrew. "Maybe we shouldn't . . . ."

"Rubbish," yelled Dave. "I've done it hundreds of times. You're scared."

"I'm not!" Andrew yelled back, watching him climb higher and higher.

"Scaredy, scaredy!" Dave's voice floated down. It was almost lost against the sound of the gulls and the sea. Andrew started to climb. He pulled himself up, puffing and panting. He had scraped his knee on the rock.

"Not far now," Dave laughed. "We have to climb round this big rock. I'll go first." He stood up on the ledge and, holding on with his fingers, started to edge himself round the rock.

Andrew looked down. The beach seemed a long way off. "Be careful," he called to Dave.

"It's easy," Dave shouted back. Suddenly a bird, startled by his voice, shot out of the cave, screeching a warning. Dave jumped back, his fingers slipped and before he could stop himself, he slid down the rock face, tumbled over and fell on to a narrow ledge.

Andrew leaned over to try and see what had happened.

"Dave, Dave!" he yelled. But there was no answer.

He looked round, but there was no one in sight on the beach or on the cliffs. Should he go for help, or stay with his friend? He started to climb down to the ledge where Dave lay. He edged slowly back and down, and then found he could go no further that way, so he had to climb up and start again. At last, after what seemed a long time, he reached the ledge.

"Are you all right?" he asked.

Dave moaned. "I've hurt my leg," he said. "I think it's broken."

Andrew looked down. They were not so far from the bottom of the cliff now, but the rocks they had walked round were covered with water. The tide was coming in, and the wind was getting stronger, blowing rain clouds from the sea.

"Help! Help!" he shouted, but his voice was lost in the wind.

Out at sea a little blue boat tossed through the waves towards them. Andrew pulled off his red anorak and waved it above his head. The boat swung round and headed back.

"He must have seen us," he shouted, shaking Dave's shoulder. "He must have!" But the boat was making for the harbour.

"He'd be picking up lobster pots," said Dave. "He's gone home for tea."

Andrew sat down on the ledge and waited. The clouds had covered the sun and it was beginning to get cold. Dave moaned and shivered.

"Don't move," Andrew told him. "Stay where you are and try to keep warm." He wrapped his red anorak round Dave, then sat back. There was no one out at sea now. The little boat had gone. The water was cold and grey, with white waves splashing at the cliff beneath them.

Andrew sat like that for a long time. It was getting late. Back at the house they would be looking for him. He stood up and stamped his feet and shouted for help, but there was no one on the cliff to hear him. He sat with his back against the rocks and started counting, very slowly, to see how far he could go.

"Two hundred and five, two hundred and six . . ." Then he stopped. The little blue boat was heading back out from the harbour. Perhaps it had seen them and was coming to lift them off. He stood up shouting and waving again, but his voice was drowned out by a sound even louder than the sea.

From behind him, over the top of the cliff, came a great rush of noise and wind. It seemed to snatch the breath from him and push him back against the rock. The yellow helicopter slid out and hung above his head, closer than he had ever seen it before.

A man in a white helmet was leaning from the open hatch, waving at him. "Don't move!" he yelled. "I'm coming down."

He swung down slowly, twisting on the end of a rope. The yellow flashing light of the helicopter shone on his goggles and helmet. Andrew crouched beside Dave to make room for him on the ledge. He

swung over and very gently stepped on to the space beside them. He seemed huge in his green flying suit and life jacket.

"Hi!" he shouted. "Just passing so I thought I'd drop in. Want a lift?"

Then he noticed that Dave had hurt himself. "We'll get you up first," he said to Andrew, "and I'll come back down with a stretcher."

He pulled the rope across and fastened the harness round Andrew.

"Now," he said, "there's nothing to be afraid of. Hold on to me and we're off."

He waved an arm and they swung suddenly up and out from the cliff. The helicopter lifted slightly and they twisted round. Andrew swallowed hard and shut his eyes. The noise grew louder until it was deafening, then suddenly he was swung round and pulled backwards into the helicopter, and the man had vanished back down again with a stretcher for Dave.

Andrew was strapped into a seat opposite the doorway. He sat gasping for breath, hardly able to believe what had happened. The man standing by the open door turned and smiled.

"I'm Ian, the winch operator," he shouted. "We'll soon have your pal up. What's your name?"

Andrew stared at him, and at the two pilots up front in the cramped cabin. It seemed so small and dark, and so noisy. He shook his head.

"Andrew," he said, but his voice sounded funny.

"It's OK," Ian shouted. "You're safe now. We'll have you home in no time." And he was right.

Three days later, just before the end of the holiday, Andrew and his Mum and Dad went to visit Dave in hospital. He was very much better, hopping about on a plaster cast and boasting about his adventures to the others in the ward.

Then there was one last visit to make. They drove out to the airfield to say goodbye and thank you to the helicopter crew. The big yellow Sea King stood silently on the runway beside the shed where the crew waited for emergency calls.

Andrew thanked them all and they gave him a squadron badge and a rescue sticker to put on his schoolbag after the holidays.

"Support Your Local Rescue Service," it said. "Get Lost!"

Andrew laughed. "I'll see you all next year," he shouted as they drove off.

"Well, you drop in on us next time," a pilot shouted back. "We prefer it that way!"

Canals in Scotland

In the story about the Crinan Canal, Anne explained how a lock works. You can see on these diagrams what she meant. Draw your own diagrams of a boat coming back 'downhill' through this lock.

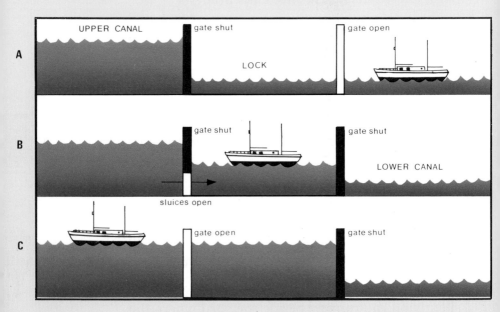

A

UPPER CANAL   gate shut   gate open

LOCK

B

gate shut   gate shut

LOWER CANAL

C

sluices open   gate open   gate shut

How a lock works:
A   Boat just before entering lock.
B   Water level in lock rising.
C   Boat raised to upper part of canal.

Imagine taking a boat through this series of eight locks, known as 'Neptune's Staircase', at Banavie on the Caledonian Canal.

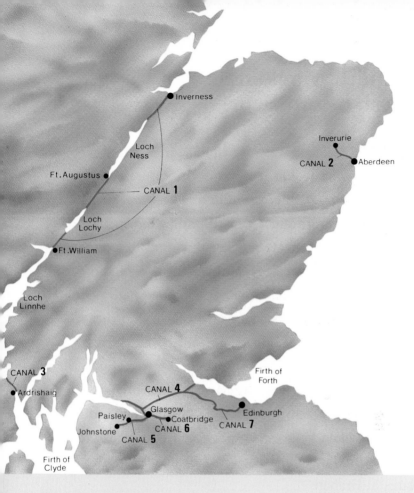

This map shows the location of the seven main canals in Scotland. Can you name them correctly from the following list?

Forth and Clyde Canal
Monkland Canal
Edinburgh and Glasgow Union Canal
Glasgow, Paisley and Johnstone Canal
Aberdeenshire Canal
Crinan Canal
Caledonian Canal

Some parts of these canals no longer exist. Find out more about your nearest canal from the local library. (If you live near Linlithgow, the Union Canal Society Museum has displays telling of the history and use of canals.)

Kenneth Mackenzie
–the Brahan Seer

Kenneth Mackenzie was no ordinary man. He was able to tell what would happen in the future. By some strange power he was able to see events which would happen both during his lifetime, and many years after his death. Because of this gift he became known as the Brahan Seer, and was respected and feared by many people.

He was born in the seventeenth century on the island of Lewis, the Long Island, in the far north-west of Scotland. His home was a cottage at Uig, built on land that belonged to the Mackenzie clan. Kenneth and his family were part of that clan and he knew that when he grew up he would go to work for the clan chieftain, the great Lord Seaforth, on his estates at Brahan.

Here are some of the events he foretold that have come true since his death.

The day will come when Tomnahurich will be under lock and key, and the fairies secured within.

Tomnahurich is a Gaelic word. In English it means the Hill of the Fairies, and for many years people had believed that there were indeed fairies living on Tomnahurich Hill, near Inverness. About two hundred years after Kenneth's death, the hilltop became a cemetery and a fence with a locked gate was built around it. It was a well-known fact in Kenneth's day that fairies could not pass through iron, so that once the gate was closed for the night they were of course trapped within.

The clans will flee their native country before an army of sheep.

When Kenneth was alive the Highland clans were strong warlike people. The clan chieftains owned much of the land and had great wealth and power. It must have seemed impossible that this would ever change. And yet, about one hundred years after his death, the clans, led by Prince Charles Edward Stuart, were defeated by the English armies. The power of the clans was broken and gradually their land was taken by English landowners. The landowners found that they could keep sheep on the hillsides that had once been farmed. The land could not support both sheep and people, so many Highlanders were driven out of their homes. Many died and others crossed the

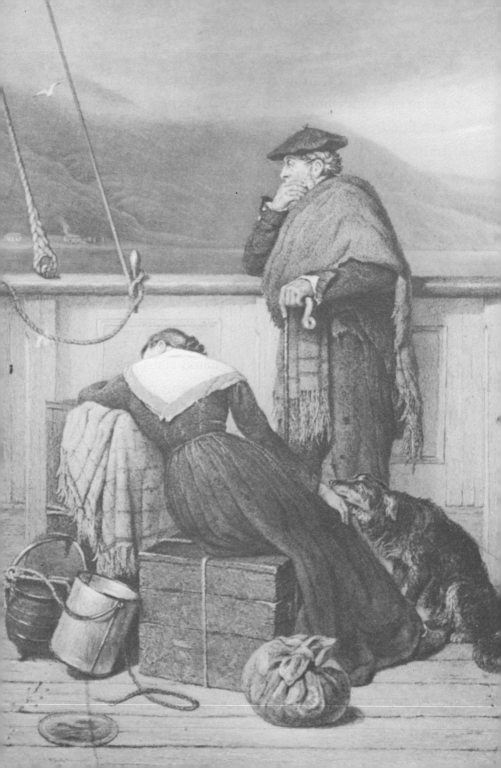

sea to Canada, America and Australia, taking with them their stories, songs and music. This period, one of the saddest in Scotland's history, became known as the Highland Clearances.

Ships will pass and repass Tomnahurich Hill.

This must have seemed a very strange idea at the time, as Tomnahurich Hill was nowhere near the sea. Many years later, though, when Scotland began to trade with countries across the Atlantic Ocean, the Caledonian Canal was built. This cut right across the country, linking the lochs of the Great Glen, taking ships from the east to the west coast of Scotland. At one stretch the canal passes Tomnahurich Hill, and so what Kenneth foresaw has indeed come true.

A cow shall give birth to a calf in the uppermost chamber of Fairburn Tower.

During Kenneth's lifetime, Fairburn was a fine castle that belonged to the Mackenzie family. Men must have laughed at this story, yet it did come true. The family who lived in Fairburn lost their money, and gradually the castle became a ruin. Many years later a local farmer used the tower, which still had a roof, as a store-room. The walls were still strong, and the upper rooms dry, so he kept straw there. Some of the straw had been scattered on the stone staircase while it was being taken up. A cow found it and, following the trail, ate her way up the stairs to the upper room. The farmer naturally did not want her eating all his straw and tried to get her back down again. But she was about to give birth to a calf so he had to leave her where she was. The calf was safely born shortly after, and some days later both it and the cow were brought back down by the farmer.

These stories and many, many more have been told about Kenneth Mackenzie. It was believed that his power came from a magic stone that was given to his mother when he was a baby. The stone was round and smooth, with a hole through the centre. It was said that when Kenneth looked through the hole he could see the future. Just before his death he threw the stone into the waters of a loch near Brahan and said that it would remain there until it was found by an old hunch-backed man. It has never been seen since.

Here is a story about how Kenneth's mother was given the stone.

The Magic Stone

There was once a young woman called Morag
Mackenzie who lived on the Long Island of Lewis,
far to the north-west of Scotland.

Life was difficult on the Long Island and Morag
and her husband worked hard to feed and clothe
themselves. They were happy, though, living a
simple life of farming and fishing. Their happiness
was made perfect when a son was born to Morag.

"We shall call him Kenneth," said his father, "and
as he grows up, I will teach him to farm and fish,
and to follow me."

But this was not good enough for Morag. She
thought her child was the most beautiful she had ever
seen. Even as a baby he seemed different from the
other children of the village. They had fair hair and
blue eyes that sparkled like the summer sea, but
Kenneth was dark. His hair was thick and black, his
eyes were brown like the dark deep lochs of the
moorland. The other children laughed and smiled.
Kenneth, even as a baby, was a still, quiet child.

"He is different," said his mother to herself. She
gazed into his dark brown eyes, that looked full of
faraway thoughts.

"He will be a great man one day," she said to her

husband. "He will not be a farmer or fisherman. A day will come when our son will be famous. People everywhere will know of him."

Her husband laughed. "To be a great man," he said, "Kenneth would need to have power over other

Morag is spinning with her distaff, which is a stick with prongs to hold sheep's wool. The wool is attached to a heavy weight which spins when it is dropped, pulling the wool into long threads.

men, and he will never have that. He is only the son of a simple farmer."

Morag smiled and said nothing, but still she had the dream in her heart.

One summer, when Kenneth was very small, Morag took their cattle to the summer shieling on the hillside above the church. Each winter the village folk kept their few cows and sheep indoors, and each summer as the young grass grew green and fresh, they were driven out to graze. While the men farmed their small fields, or went to the fishing, some of the women went to the shieling with their animals.

They took the smaller children with them, and spent the long summer days on the sunny hills. They passed the time spinning wool from the sheep on their distaffs, or knitting it into warm clothing for the long winter. Through the long, light nights they slept in the little shieling huts.

One night Morag could not sleep. The day had been long and hot, and the shieling was stuffy. She sat up in the half-dark and looked around. By her side Kenneth, tired out by playing with the other children, slept quietly. The other women and children were all sound asleep. Morag lifted her distaff and some wool, and folded her cloak around her.

She pulled aside the heavy curtain that covered the

door and stepped out into the cool summer night. The sky is never really dark at that time of year in the north. Morag walked in the soft grey light down the hillside. The grass was cool and damp under her bare feet. The cows were still, dark shapes, like statues, around her.

Her feet swished through the long grass, down towards the churchyard. On the other side of it the cold waters of a small loch lay still and silvery. As she walked she felt, rather than saw, shapes moving round her. She stopped and stood peering in the dark. In the churchyard the smooth green grass above the graves seemed to be open, and soft grey ghosts were floating across the hillside. There were old men and women, young people and children among them. Morag stared in wonder. She hid by the wall and watched for hours as the ghosts came and went around her. As the long night wore on towards morning, she saw that all the graves were covered over again, except one. That grave stood on its own in a corner of the churchyard, and the stone beside it was so old that Morag could not read the name on it. Greatly daring, she crept forward and laid her distaff by the open grave. It was said that no spirit could enter a grave while a distaff lay there. She knelt by the stone and waited.

At last, in the early light of dawn, there came a voice. "Lift thy distaff from off my grave and let me enter the house of the dead."

Morag looked up. At her side there stood a young woman. She was tall and beautiful. Her long white hair hung in two thick plaits down to her waist. Her silver-white dress seemed to be made of mist and water. Around her bare feet trailed soft green seaweed.

"The other spirits returned long since," said Morag. "Tell me why you are so late?"

"My journey was longer than theirs," said the young woman. "And now I am tired and must rest."

"But who are you?" asked Morag. "You must tell me that too."

"I was a princess of Norway," said the ghost, "the daughter of a great king. I lived by the sea and more than anything I loved to swim and to be free like the sea creatures. One summer I was drowned and my body was found at last on your island. I lie buried here, but I must return to my home in Norway. That is why I am later than the others."

"A sad story," said Morag. "I will take my distaff. You may return to your rest."

"There are few who know my story," said the princess. "Few who are brave enough to do what you did. Because of that I shall give you a prize not given to many. With it your son shall become a great man, and his name will be known and feared far and wide."

Morag jumped to her feet. "I knew it!" she said. "Tell me, what is this treasure?"

"No treasure," said the princess. "It is a stone."

"A stone?" Morag was puzzled.

"Go down to the shore of the loch," said the princess, "and walk to the edge of the water. As you turn to face the rising sun you will see at your feet a smooth blue stone. Through the middle of the stone there is a hole. Take it and keep it for your son."

"But how will that make him great?" asked Morag. "The beach is covered with stones. Why should that one be different?"

"Because that one has power," said the princess. "If your son looks through the hole in that stone he will be able to see the future. He will have the

gift of knowing what is to come." She smiled sadly and nodded her head.

"There indeed lies power," whispered Morag.

"Both the good and the bad," said the princess faintly. "Now, good woman, remove your distaff and bring me to my rest."

So Morag picked up her distaff. The princess faded from her sight and the grave lay still and green.

Morag stood gazing around her at the quiet churchyard. "I am surely dreaming," she said.

Then, remembering the princess's story, she ran down to the water's edge. She lifted her face to the morning wind. There, as the rising sun laid a path of gold at her feet, she found the blue stone. She lifted it gently from the beach, and brushed the sand from it. It seemed to glow with a deep blue light. Morag wrapped the stone in her cloak, gathered up her distaff and returned to the shieling.

For many years she kept the stone hidden. Then, when Kenneth was old enough, she told him the story of the princess and gave it to him.

As the princess had said, Kenneth Mackenzie grew up to be a great man who could see the future, both the good and the bad. People came from far and wide to hear his words and to marvel at the farmer's son who had such wonderful and fearful powers.

The Paddle Steamer

Whooooooooo! Whoooooooooooo!

The siren of the old paddle steamer echoes over the still summer sea. It can be heard everywhere in the little seaside town.

People put down the Sunday newspapers and listen. "Summer's back," they say. "Here she comes."

Children playing in the back gardens whoop in answer. Whooooooooo! Whhhhoooooooooo!

A plume of white steam gushes from the whistle high on the black and red funnel. The old ship takes a wide sweep round towards the pier. She sails in slowly. Her wake trails behind her like crisp white lace on a green silk cloak. Her head is wreathed in a veil of soft grey smoke. White seagulls dance around like bridesmaids.

"She's coming! She's coming!" screams every child on the pier.

"Of course she is."

"Keep back from the edge."

"Watch what you're doing there."

Mothers and fathers push round, grabbing eager children. They drag picnic bags, plastic raincoats and prams, shouting warnings. Underneath the grown-up worries, they too feel the thrill of the old ship.

She slows, the paddles churning gently to a halt. She is still some way out from the pier. Will she ever come in?

Little waves slap from her sides across the water to leap against the huge black posts beneath the pier. The steady thump-thump of the engine seems to beat through everyone. The ship slowly slides in to stop in exactly the right place.

The heavy wooden gang-planks clatter down, linking land to sea. The red paint of the handrails shines bright and glossy for a new summer season. The wooden treads are worn smooth and dark by a thousand feet of summers past.

People rush up from the pier, crowding to get on board. They are eager to join those already there, the holiday-makers leaning on the rail or sprawled across the wooden seats on the deck. They have been on the boat for the past hour and have explored every corner. They feel like old sailors. They nod in passing to brown-faced seamen pulling on the thick ropes. They know what to expect as gang-planks are hauled back on board. Engines throb faster and faster, and the sea churns beneath the huge paddles.

Ropes are thrown from the pier into the water to be pulled back up on the deck. They come up black and dripping. The pier slides swiftly past and away

from the ship. Two small boys sitting at the end look up from their fishing lines and wave goodbye. They are left alone with an old newspaper that blows across the empty pier. The steamer is on her way.

The newcomers, puffing and panting, search for a space. Bags are parked and coats spread out to make a family place. Hats tied down firmly with bright silk scarves, mothers settle down to enjoy the sun.

Some passengers are curious to see how the steamer works. They go below to stare at the engines. The huge, dark, stuffy, oil-smelling cave in the heart of the ship pounds with noise. People stand round the painted railings staring down into the moving mass of metal. Polished brass levers and shining silver pistons move together in rhythm to drive their little world on towards the next harbour.

This small ship is the last of a long, proud line of paddle steamers. Others like her, built in Clydeside shipyards, left their Scottish home to sail to far-off ports. In places like Hong Kong, Buenos Aires and Bombay the same engines thumped and chugged in busy harbours.

Paddle steamers carried British goods overseas and brought back tea and sugar, gold and diamonds.

Wartime evacuation from Gravesend by paddle steamer, 1939.

They were used in wartime to defend the coast and to carry soldiers. Some of the ships never came back and still lie buried beneath the seas.

In a dark corner sits the engineer. A small square man in blue overalls, he smiles quietly to himself and puffs at his pipe. His eyes are everywhere, watching the clocks and dials above his head, watching the rise and fall of the engine, watching the passengers watching him. With only a dirty rag and a large spanner, he sits like a wizard at the feet of his great magical monster.

Above his head children run on the sunlit decks, screaming and free as gulls. Up ladders and down stairways they go, in and out of doorways. The sudden shift of the floor beneath their feet or the wind snatching at skirts and hats, become part of a new game. They peer into lifeboats. They stand and stare in at the door of the café. They try out the toilets and drop toffee papers down the ventilators to see what will happen. Nothing ever does. Like an invading army they take over the ship.

"Come and see what's up here."

"Look at the size of these ropes!"

"What's that bit for Dad?"

"I don't know. Ask your Mum."

Mothers and fathers search their memories for half-forgotten words. They try to explain how an engine works, where a doorway leads, to children who cannot stand still long enough to listen.

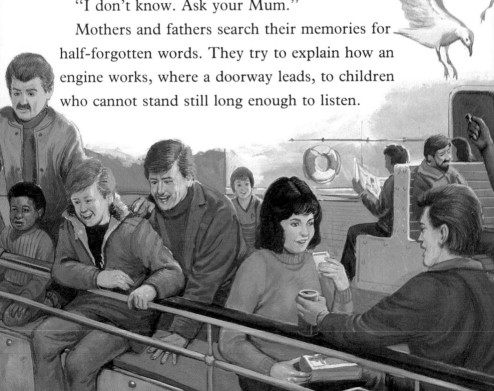

People turn away at last from the hot stuffy smell of the engines to the clean sea-blown air.

"Fancy a cup of tea?"

"What did you put in the sandwiches?"

"Have we got orange juice or lemonade?"

"Sit down! Stop jumping about! You'll spill something!"

All over the ship empty stomachs rumble. Breakfast was a long time ago and everyone was too excited to eat anyway. Families come back, as if at a signal, to their own places. Bags are emptied and parcels opened. A plastic box of sandwiches is passed round. The wrapping paper flaps like flags in the stiff breeze. The seagulls dive and swoop towards the decks with a new interest.

"Eat up your crusts and your hair will grow curly."

"But Gran, I don't want curly hair!"

And for once nobody insists. Crusts are thrown to the gulls. They catch and swallow in mid-air. And all the time their bright beady eyes are searching for more.

Empty paper cake-cases and half-chewed straws are dumped in the ashtrays. Lemonade is drunk from the bottle. On a ship anything goes.

The last crumb is licked from a plate, the last sandwich is shared out. The last drops of lemonade slurp noisily in the bottom of the bottle. Tea is over. Litter is tidied away, bags are packed and flasks emptied.

"Would you like the last cup of tea, Gran?"

"Well ... all right then."

The children grab their parents and drag them round the ship.

"Come and see what's down here Mum."

"I'll tell her first."

"No I found it."

Everyone is feeling cross and tired in the heat.

"Who'd like an ice cream?" Mum, as usual, has the answer. Arguments are forgotten. The ice cream, hot and sticky, melts on dirty hands.

"If you bite the bottom off a cone, you can suck it through."

"Don't do that, you'll drip it all down your tee-shirt." Sticky fingers are wiped, faces mopped. The sweet cold ice cream joins the salt wind and the hot oil of the engines in a smell you can taste. On deck, dark smoke blows down from the funnel, adding another flavour.

Grans and grandads remember other summers long ago when they were children. Another time, another world, but the tastes and smells are still the same. Will these children now playing on the decks remember this when they are old?

Whhhhhooooooo! Whooooooooo! Another plume of white steam, like a huge feather, comes from the whistle. Across the water lies another pier, another harbour. The ship tilts to one side as children, fathers, mothers and crew alike gather to watch.

The tiny toy houses, sparkling white against the hillside, grow larger. On the pier another group of people stands waiting. They grab at bags, coats and children, ready to storm up the gang-plank.

"She's coming. She's coming."

Every child screams with delight. They leap and dance on the pier to see seagulls swoop low over the old ship as she slides gently in towards them.

Glasgow Museum of Transport

If you go to the Glasgow Museum of Transport you can see trams, bicycles, cars, trains, horse-drawn vehicles and a collection of model ships – all telling the story of land and sea transport. Some examples are shown on these pages.

Scotland has over three hundred museums and galleries, visited by almost five million people each year. Apart from the Glasgow Museum, there are many others which have collections related to transport. Perhaps one of them is near you?

Some examples:

Aberdeen	Maritime Museum	*Hamilton*	Hamilton District Museum
Aberlady	Myreton Motor Museum	*Kingussie*	Highland Folk Museum
Boat of Garten	Strathspey Railway		
Doune	Motor Museum	*Kirkcaldy*	Industrial Museum
Dundee	Central Museum and Art Gallery	*Linlithgow*	Union Canal Society Museum
Edinburgh	Braidwood and Rushbrook Museum	*North Berwick*	Museum of Flight
	Royal Scottish Museum	*Orkney*	Stromness Museum
		Shetland	Shetland Museum
Falkirk	Falkirk Museum Scottish Railway Preservation Society		

The 'Gordon Highlander', a locomotive used in north-east Scotland from 1920, when it was built, to 1966, when it was presented to the Museum.

A Glasgow tram, built in 1924, as it was fitted out in the 1928 modernisation. These trams seated 59 passengers (21 below and 38 on top). 10 more could stand in the lower saloon.

If you had lived a hundred years ago, what would your favourite form of transport have been? Draw or paint a picture of yourself making a 'historical journey'.

The oldest cycle in the world.

Nature and the Arts in Scotland

Robert Burns, poet (1759–96)

Robert Burns was born on the 25th of January in the year 1759. On the night of his birth the storms raged so fiercely round the little stone cottage his father had built for the family that the end wall came crashing down around them. Nature welcomed Robert to the world with a wild and stormy fanfare!

> Our monarch's hindmost year but ane,
> > Was five and twenty days begun,
> 'Twas then a blast o' Januar' win',
> > Blew hansel in on Robin.

His father and grandfather before him worked on the land. As Robert and his brothers grew up, they were expected to join their father working as farmers. To Robert, who loved the countryside, that must have seemed the most natural thing to do. At the same time however, his father made sure that the boys received the best education he could afford to give them. Robert was lucky. He had a fine teacher named John Murdoch, who inspired in his pupil a love of books, poetry and music that remained with him all his life.

hindmost, last   *ane*, one   *hansel*, gift

It was this love of poetry, combined with his feeling for the fields, woods and rivers of his native Ayrshire, that led Robert to discover his own special talent, for which he is still remembered.

Aft hae I roved by bonie Doon,
    To see the rose and woodbine twine,
And ilka bird sang o' its love,
    And fondly sae did I o' mine.

Poets before Robert had written about the countryside, but their words were stiff and stilted. They worked according to rules that said how long a poem should be, what words should express the feeling of the poet, what patterns of rhyme should be used. They wrote as scholars, at a desk, working to produce a perfect exercise in poetry.

Robert was the exact opposite. He wrote as a man who had spent long summer days working from dawn till dusk, harvesting corn and barley. He wrote as a farmer who had trudged behind a plough through the thickening mud of an autumn field, and stopping from time to time to scribble a line or two in his notebook. He wrote as a neighbour, who shared the lives of the people around him, and who joined with them in laughter and sadness.

ilka, every   *sae*, so

Birthplace of Burns
at Alloway,
Ayrshire

Robert Burns,
by Alexander Nasmyth

Brig O'Doon,
where Tam O'Shanter's
mare, Meg, lost
her tail.

Most important of all he wrote, not in the language of the scholar, but in the words of ordinary country people. He expressed his love of nature as simply as he greeted a fellow-farmer in the market place. Because of that his poems come alive, even today, with a fresh earthy sparkle.

> A rosebud by my early walk,
> Adown a corn enclosed bawk,
> Sae gently bent its thorny stalk,
>   All on a dewy morning.

We can come closest to Robert himself in the poem *The Cottar's Saturday Night*. The cottar himself is said to be a portrait of Robert's father, and we are drawn into the closeness of the family and feel with him what it was like to sit round the cottage fireside on a cold winter evening.

> His wee bit ingle, blinkin' bonilie,
> His clean hearth-stane, his thrifty wifie's smile,
> The lisping infant, prattling on his knee,
> Does a' his weary carking cares beguile,
> And makes him quite forget his labour and his toil.

bawk, bank   *ingle*, fireplace   *carking*, anxious

Robert worked long and hard as a farmer. Because of poverty and the hardship of his life his health was never good and, sadly, he died still a young man. But while he lived he had listened to the birds and animals; he had watched seasons come and go, changing the countryside around him. And he had poured his love and warmth and sense of fun into the poems and songs he wrote.

Robert was an ordinary working man who cared deeply for his friends and his home. But because he had an extraordinary gift and could put his feelings into words, we, and many other people around the world today, can still share them with him.

David Wilkie, RA, painter (1785–1841)

The young man sat at the back of the church, his head bowed, his hands in his lap beneath the pew. From time to time he would glance up at the people around him and watch them closely for a minute or two. Then his eyes would drop again, and his face become a study in serious concentration.

To the people of Pitlessie, listening to their parish minister, it must have seemed as if the minister's son was paying a great deal of attention to his father's sermon. But young David Wilkie was doing no such thing. He was drawing – as usual.

His hands, hidden beneath the edge of the pew, held a notebook and pencil. David was sketching the faces of his father's congregation. He drew the old men and women, nodding off to sleep as the long sermon wore on. He drew the girls in their Sunday bonnets, smiling across at the young men who would walk home with them afterwards. He drew the children, fidgeting to be out in the sunshine, nudging and winking at each other under the disapproving eyes of their parents.

As long as anyone could remember, from the time David Wilkie had been one of these small children himself, he had drawn pictures. If he could find a piece of paper and something that would make a mark on it, he was happy. As David grew older his father realised that the boy would never be a minister, but that he did have a real talent for art. So at the age of fourteen he was sent to school in Edinburgh.

He soon proved his father's judgment to be correct. In Edinburgh, among good teachers, David quickly learned how to paint. So well did he progress that by the age of nineteen he was recognised in society as a very talented young man, with a particular gift for painting portraits.

Self-portrait by David Wilkie

David might have stayed in Edinburgh, making a name for himself. He might have become just another fashionable artist, skilled at producing elegant, flattering pictures of the ladies and gentlemen who had the time to sit for him, and the money to pay for his paintings. He did neither of these.

David Wilkie did not really want to spend his time painting portraits for the gentry. He wanted to paint pictures of the ordinary people he had grown up with. He wanted to show how they lived and dressed, how they worked, and how they enjoyed themselves. So he went back to Pitlessie and drew the faces of his father's congregation.

Over the weeks and months he collected a hundred and forty of these portraits of ordinary village people, and put them all together in a painting called *Pitlessie Fair*. The local people are all there, laughing, talking, singing and enjoying themselves at an open-air fair in the village. Their faces are painted so perfectly that you feel you know these people very well. Perhaps it was David's way of saying 'thank you' to the many friends of his childhood and youth, in any event the painting made him famous. People heard of it and flocked to see it and marvel at the talents of the young man. They admired the obvious honesty and affection with which he painted his fellow villagers.

His career prospered after that. He went to London where he was accepted as a member of the Royal Academy, and his paintings were sold for a great deal of money. David Wilkie RA was very much in demand as a portrait painter of the rich and famous, but he never lost touch with his first love.

He returned several times to Scotland and continued to paint pictures of the ordinary everyday life of the people.

The Cottar's Saturday Night, illustrating the poem by Robert Burns, shows a little family gathered round the table, listening intently while father reads from the family Bible. The faces are quiet and thoughtful and tired, but there is a feeling of warmth and gentleness, of a close family group. In *The Penny Wedding* the same ordinary working people have come together to share what must have been one of the great events of their lives. They are celebrating the wedding of a much-loved young couple, and in that celebration perhaps forgetting for a while the hard work and poverty of their everyday existence.

In both pictures it is clear that David Wilkie drew his inspiration, not from fine clothes and jewels, but from his love for the ordinary, honest working people of his native Scotland.

Felix Mendelssohn, composer (1809–47)

The small boat pulled away from the steamer and headed towards the lonely island. Sailors hauled on the huge wooden oars, grunting and puffing against the force of the wind. The boat rose and fell on the great surging swell that rolled in from the Atlantic Ocean and broke in a froth of cream round the black rocks.

"Look, Felix, look! There's the cave. The size – the magnificence of it! Look, quickly ..." Carl grabbed his friend's arm and shook it. Ahead of them Fingal's Cave opened, a great gaping mouth in the sheer cliff face of the island.

But Felix sat huddled in the stern of the boat, his face as green as the sea around him. He had been sick since the steamer had left Tobermory harbour very early on that wet and windy morning. He had become colder and more miserable the further out they sailed towards the little island of Staffa. He had watched his friend Carl, who never seemed to be upset by anything, enjoy breakfast on that heaving deck and wondered how it was possible. Felix Mendelssohn had no stomach for breakfast or sailing, that was certain!

But he was not alone in this. Most of the other

passengers, like himself, huddled cold and shivering in the small boat. They had only decided to come ashore on the island because it seemed the only solid point in a heaving, tossing world. Now, clinging to the sides of the boat, drawing towards the huge black rocky columns of Staffa, who knew what they were thinking!

"Why, oh why, did I ever come here?"

"Would that I had stayed in bed."

"If I return alive, never, never again will I set foot on board a ship!"

Felix pulled down the collar of his coat and lifted his pale face to stare at the island. He watched for a long time and slowly forgot how cold and miserable he had felt. Through his head was running a piece of music, an insistent, gentle theme, rising and falling like the waves. It was a piece of music that told, more vividly than he could ever put into words, of his feeling for the wild northern seas and the lonely islands of the Hebrides.

Felix Mendelssohn was a German composer. He had discovered a love of music at the age of three, when his mother had taught him how to play the piano in the parlour of their comfortable home in Hamburg. By the time he was twelve, Felix was not only playing but also writing his own music.

He loved nature and drew much of his inspiration from what he saw around him. He once wrote, 'It is in pictures, ruins and natural surroundings that I find most music.'

Not long before his visit to Scotland he had become famous for his overture to the play *A Midsummer Night's Dream*, by William Shakespeare. Much of this magical, delicate music was written in the gardens of the Mendelssohn family's new home in Berlin.

And now, at the age of twenty, he had come on

holiday to Scotland with his old friend Carl
Klingemann. The weather, as so often happens in
Scotland, was dreadful. The inns and houses where
they stayed were not very good. Travelling on the
poorly-made roads was not always easy. However,
they still enjoyed themselves enormously, and sent
home letters describing their travels. Felix, who was
a fine artist, sketched the countryside through which
they passed and Carl wrote a poem for each drawing.
They became the perfect souvenirs of happy memories.

The most lasting memory of that holiday, and the
one for which it will always be remembered, was that
piece of music which echoed and re-echoed through
his head as Felix clung to the small boat off Staffa.
Gradually the little tune grew, to become a great
sweeping picture, a poem in sound. At first Felix
called it *The Lonely Island*, and then, perhaps as it
grew in grandeur and swept on in his mind, the
memories of other places came back to him and it
became known as *The Hebrides Overture*. We also
know it today as *Fingal's Cave*.

Felix Mendelssohn spent only a few days of his life
in Scotland during that holiday, and never returned
afterwards, but the music he left us is still one of the
most haunting and moving descriptions of the wild
and lonely islands of the west coast.

Felix Mendelssohn

Like Robert Burns and David Wilkie, Felix
Mendelssohn looked around him and drew his
inspiration from what he found there.

Burns, in his poems, gave us the farms and
woodlands of his native Ayrshire. Wilkie's paintings
are a fascinating record of country people and how
they lived. Mendelssohn's music speaks of the sea
and the lonely islands of the Hebrides.

Together, each using his own art, they have left a
vivid and enchanting picture of Scotland, the country
they loved so much.

Forward Search

"Carol!" There was a shout from the kitchen. "Will you stop watching that television and come and give me a hand?"

"I'm not watching television!" Carol shouted. She sat with her eyes glued to the screen.

"Don't tell lies, miss, I can hear it," shouted back her mother.

"It's the video," said Carol. She got up from the floor and walked backwards to the door. Her eyes were still watching the pictures on the screen. Her mother came into the room.

"Stop messing about," she said, "and come and do something."

"Coming," sighed Carol. She stopped the machine, and switched it off.

"That thing will take over your life one of these days," moaned her mother, going back to the kitchen.

Carol made a face, and followed her.

At tea-time her father came in, excited. "I've hired a video camera for next month," he said. "We can take it to the Gala and make our own film. What do you think?"

"Great!" said Carol. "Can I use it?"

"If you're careful," he said. "These things cost money."

"I should think they do," said her mother. "But it'll be good to have a film of the last Gala Day."

"It won't be the last," said Carol. "There's bound to be another field they can use next year."

For the past thirty years the annual village Gala Day had been held on the disused wartime airfield down by the school. The land had now been sold. A housing estate was soon to replace the old concrete huts and empty runways. The Gala would have to move elsewhere.

For weeks Carol and her class had been busy at school preparing fancy dress costumes. She was going to be dressed as a robot. Her class was decorating a lorry to look like a spaceship. She spent hours working at her costume, sticking on egg boxes and cardboard tubes. When the whole thing was sprayed with silver paint it looked very good.

The weather for once was dry and sunny for the Gala. From early in the morning the road to the airfield was busy. People came and went with home baking, flowers, vegetables, last-minute jumble. There was a feeling of excitement everywhere. Even the red, white and blue flags seemed brighter.

All day Carol and her father filmed the scene.

They filmed the races. They filmed the fancy dress competition. The spaceship came second to a Dracula's castle, complete with black bats and green lights. They filmed the tug-of-war, the treasure hunt, and the tombola. At the end of the afternoon they filmed the prize-giving.

Everyone they met wanted to know what they were doing. "Can we come and see it?" they asked.

Two weeks later, at Carol's house, they saw it. The video tape was great fun. Carol thought the whole village seemed to be there – crowded into their small front room. Everyone roared with laughter, pointing to each other on the small screen.

"Do you remember that?"

"Look at our Margaret!"

"Who's that behind the tent?"

At last they finished their teas and coffees and left. Carol stood in the smoky front room alone, looking at the TV screen. Her parents were out at the front gate saying goodbye to the last visitors.

Carol smiled to herself, remembering the custard pie competition. She leaned over the back of the chair and pressed the Forward Search button to find it again on the tape.

The film speeded through. Somehow it seemed slightly faster than usual. The images were more blurred. There was something different about the custard pie scene. Carol stopped the machine and ran it at normal speed. No, there was nothing different. Everyone was there just as they had been. She shrugged and pressed the Forward Search button again.

The film ran through fast. Yes, it *was* different. Quite definitely! It was duller. There seemed to be fewer people. And there was something yellow in the background that Carol couldn't really remember having seen. There was a hand reaching for a box. That must have been the lucky dip, Carol thought. She couldn't remember having seen it first time. But then everyone had been laughing and joking. She might have missed it.

Suddenly, as the hand reached towards the box, the screen went blank.

Before Carol had time to do anything the film started running again. Had she imagined it? Had the screen really been blank? She stopped the tape, ran it back, and pressed the button. The film ran through at normal speed. She was looking at the tug-of-war. There was no sign of a lucky dip box.

"Time for bed, Carol." Her mother came into the room.

"Mum!" she said. "I just want to see this again."

"Not tonight," said her mother.

Her father came back in, switched off the machine, and took out the video tape. "Great, isn't it?" he said.

"Mmm," said Carol, not sure what to say. She went off to bed very puzzled.

She watched the tape again next day. The same thing happened. Run at normal speed there was the tug-of-war team, heaving and pulling. Wound back and run at fast speed on Forward Search there was definitely a difference. It was duller. There were clouds, and the ground looked quite wet. Again there was the box. Carol sat with her eyes glued to the set as the hand reached out.

Suddenly the hand stopped. It was as if someone had pressed Freeze Frame. Carol stared at the hand for what seemed like minutes, but must have been only seconds. The screen went blank. She ran the tape back and played it again at normal speed. Once again, up came the straining faces of the tug-of-war team.

When her father came home from work that night she told him what had happened.

"You've been fiddling with that thing too much," he said. "I hope you haven't broken anything." He pressed the Forward Search button and stood watching as the tape ran through.

"There it is!" shouted Carol. "That hand, and the box. Look, it's stopped again."

Her father turned and stared at her. "Carol," he said, "that's the tug-of-war team. What are you on about?"

"It hasn't stopped," said her mother. "It's running on just like it should."

"It has! It has!" yelled Carol. She couldn't bear it. She stood there staring at a blank screen.

"There's nothing wrong with it," said her father, shaking his head.

Carol ran up to her room and threw herself on the bed, crying.

Her mother got the doctor next day. He tested Carol's eyes, which were perfectly all right. He took her pulse and asked several questions which sounded stupid to her.

"I know I saw it," said Carol. "I know I did."

"Your Dad and I didn't," said her mother. She looked across at the doctor and raised her eyes in despair. He thought perhaps Carol was tired and gave her a tonic.

"Don't watch too much television for a while," he said. "It can cause eyestrain."

Carol sat on the bed after they had gone. She thumped the pillow with her fist. Her mother called from the foot of the stairs.

"I'm going down to the shops," she said. "Will you be all right on your own?"

"Of course!" shouted Carol. Anyone would think she was a baby. As soon as her mother had gone, she put the video tape back in the machine and pressed the Forward Search button. The pictures rolled through, faster and faster. She sat biting her nails, waiting for the box and the hand.

The picture froze. The hand reaching for the box stopped inches short of the lid. Carol could see the box quite plainly now. It was greenish-grey metal with a lid. It was nothing like the box they used for the lucky dip. Suddenly the screen went blank.

"No!" she shouted, standing up. The picture came back. Frozen again as before. Four times it flashed to blank, and back to the one frozen frame of the hand. Each time there was a little more detail. It was a man's hand, brown and dirty. He wore a gold signet ring on his third finger. There was a black bruise on one finger nail.

A muffled voice came from somewhere inside the machine. Or was it inside Carol's head? "It's mine."

"What's yours?" Carol shouted. "Who are you? Who are you?"

They found her lying, where she had fainted, on the living-room floor. After that her father gave the tape to someone else to keep for him.

Three months later, on a cold October day, Carol came out of the school at four o'clock. All day bulldozers had been working near the hedge in the corner of the old airfield. The noise as they moved back and forward clearing the ground seemed to become louder as the day went on. Carol had a headache.

"Come on," shouted some of the others. "Let's go and watch them."

"You go," said Carol. "I'm going home." She turned to walk down to the road alone. Suddenly she stopped. There was a voice behind her, muffled and unclear. "It's mine," it seemed to say. "It's mine."

Carol turned quickly. She was standing alone in the quiet lane. There was no one in sight.

"Wait for me!" she yelled. She ran to catch the others. Suddenly she had to be with somebody.

In the corner of the airfield the huge yellow bulldozers stood in a silent circle. The workmen crouched in front of them, looking at something.

One man knelt on the wet earth. His hand reached for a grey-green metal box. It was a workman's hand, strong, brown and dirty. One fingernail was marked black from a bruise. On the third finger was a gold signet ring.

The children crowded closer to see what the men had found.

"It's a mine! It's a mine!"

The voice screamed loud and clear at last. It was Carol's voice as she pushed through the children towards the workmen. They all turned to stare at her. The hand froze above the landmine that had lain buried for forty years in the corner of the airfield.

Queen Mary's Escape from Loch Leven Castle

I never wanted to do the job in the first place, and it was my mother's fault that I was there at all.

I'll tell you what happened. I suppose the story really started in the summer of 1567, last year. I think I was about fifteen or sixteen, though I'm not too sure about that. There are a lot of us in the family and my mother never bothers to remember birthdays. She wouldn't be able to buy us presents anyway, even if she did remember.

I'm the oldest son in the family. My father died some years ago and there's never much money for anything. We have a small farm and we manage to live off that, but it has been difficult.

We weren't always poor, because my father has proud and powerful relations. They are the Douglas family, and they own all the land where we live, by the side of Loch Leven. The castle on the island in the loch belongs to Sir William Douglas. I was named after him, but they don't call me Sir William, just plain Willy Douglas. Perhaps my father thought it would make Sir William do something to help me, but in the end it was my mother who spoke to Sir William.

It all happened because there had been fighting and trouble in the country for years. It was said that some of the lords in Edinburgh had raised an army against Queen Mary and were trying to take the throne from her.

Some of the lads from the village had gone to join the Queen's army. One of them came home last summer full of fine talk. The stories he had to tell about the Queen, and the streets of Edinburgh and the fine lords around her! I begged my mother to let me go back with him, to join the Queen's army and fight for her. But mother would have none of it, she said that was the kind of nonsense my father used to talk, and that it was time I had an honest job.

We argued about it a lot, but in the end she went to Loch Leven Castle and begged Sir William to take me into his service. He agreed to pay her enough money to help with the farm if I would promise to stay and work hard for him, so that was how I became a page in the household of Sir William Douglas.

I hated it. You would have thought living in the castle would be exciting. Well, it was anything but. I had to wait at table on Sir William and his wife and mother. I stood there for hours on end, handing round dishes and pouring wine for them. The food that I ate was never very good. There was never much left and I had to wait for it until after everyone else had eaten, so it was always cold.

The castle was cold too, cold and damp and grey, like the mists that came up from the loch. Nothing ever seemed to happen there. I sometimes thought I would have been better living in a prison, for it often seemed like that.

The ruins of Loch Leven Castle

There were times, though, when Sir William's brother George came up from Edinburgh with his friends. They were a wild lot, drinking and laughing and joking. I liked waiting at table for them, pouring the wine all night and watching the fun. Sir William didn't like them, they made too much noise for him. So George came only rarely, and then only for one or two days to see his mother. After he went away things always seemed duller than ever, and I hated it even more.

And then, last June, everything changed. I remember it was one of those lovely clear summer days, when it was almost warm in the castle. I was sitting fishing on the rocks below the gate when a boat came over from the shore. There was a man standing in it, shouting and waving. It was something about the Queen's army. It seemed that there had been a battle at a place called Carberry Hill, and she had been taken prisoner. Her army and the lords who had fought with her were scattered or imprisoned.

The messenger spent a long time that night talking with Sir William in his room. By sunrise the next morning the man had left, but for days afterwards there were people coming and going. The room at the top of the big tower was cleared out and I had to help carry in a bed and tables and chairs.

Three nights later the boat came over again, in the dark this time. There were a few soldiers, a big dark man who seemed to be in command, and some ladies. It was difficult to see in the dark, but one of them, taller and thinner than the others, looked as if she was ill. They helped her up to the tower room and left her there with the other ladies.

That night I had to wait at table on Sir William and the big dark man. He was a fine lord, right enough, but there was something about him that frightened me. I know he was not a man I would have liked to work for. He was big and strong, with hard black eyes that seemed to watch everything at once. He drank very little, but he talked, and it was then I discovered who the lady was. The big dark man told Sir William that she must be kept safely imprisoned in the castle. He said that the future of Scotland lay in Sir William's hands and that no one must be allowed to even come near the Queen. I was pouring a glass of wine for him when he said it, and I almost dropped it in his lap. To think of Queen Mary a prisoner in Loch Leven Castle!

Of course I tried to catch a glimpse of her after that. I was curious to see what a queen looked like. I took food up to the tower room every day, but I was never allowed in. I had to give it to one of her ladies at the door, because they said the Queen herself was very ill. At first they hated us all and refused to talk to me, but I took them other things besides food. One day I picked a bunch of flowers from Lady Douglas's garden, and another time I took up one of the little white kittens from the kitchens. The lady said that the Queen liked that.

Gradually they spoke to me more and more, and then one day I was at last allowed into the room to meet the Queen herself. I don't really know what I was expecting her to look like, but I'll never forget that first meeting as long as I live. She was standing

Mary Queen of Scots

by the window, looking out across the grey waters of the loch. It was late September by this time, and the weather was beginning to turn cold.

Queen Mary turned and looked at me and her face was as white as the snow on the hills. She seemed to glow in the dark corner of the room, like the pearls that Lady Douglas sometimes wore. She was tall, much taller than me and taller even than Sir William I think, with dark reddish-brown hair. She wasn't dressed like a queen, her clothes were plain and dark, but you would have known who she was for all that. She said she was tired and asked me to stay and talk to them, to amuse them, so I talked about my mother and the farm, and the things that happened in the castle.

I spent a lot of time with the Queen and her ladies after that. Sometimes I talked to them and made them laugh. Sometimes Queen Mary told me stories about her life as it was when she lived in France. She had lived at court with the French King and Queen, and had been married to the prince who would have become king. But he had died, and so she came back to Scotland. She said that was when all her troubles began. She loved France and talked a lot about the sunshine and the gardens full of fountains and flowers, and how much she wanted to go back there.

Loch Leven Castle was cold and damp, and she hated it just as much as I did.

All through the winter she talked to me about how she longed to go home to France, and of course I wanted to help her to get away from the place. By the time the spring came again we had decided what we must do. I knew that some of the women who worked in the kitchens lived on the other side of the loch and went ashore with the boatman every night. I stole two old cloaks, gave them to the Queen and one of her ladies, and helped them down to the castle gate as the kitchen women were going home for the night. Nobody stopped us or asked any questions and I chatted to them just as if they were serving-maids or laundry-women. I gave them each a bundle of dirty washing to carry ashore to make it look more real. But that was my mistake.

When the Queen was climbing into the boat she dropped her bundle, and when she reached out to pick it up again the boatman realised that she was no laundry-woman. She had beautiful hands, long and white, and he knew immediately who she was. She offered him money and a ring, but he was afraid for his life, and refused to take her ashore. He promised he wouldn't tell Sir William though, and for that she was very grateful.

We tried several times after that to think of some way to escape. One of the Queen's maids even tried jumping from a window, but she hurt her ankle. I had to find a rope to climb down and pull her back in again. We told Sir William she had fallen on the stairs, which would not have been difficult because they are very old and worn.

It began to look as though Queen Mary would never escape, and she was becoming more and more unhappy, when George Douglas came back to the castle. The Queen had dinner that night with Sir William and all the family in the hall. She enjoyed herself. It was a long time since she had met so many people, and she laughed and talked happily. I could see George Douglas watching her all the time, and when she left to go back to her room, he stood and stared after her. Her dress and jewellery were not so fine as those that Lady Douglas wore, but she was so much more beautiful. I think George Douglas fell in love with her there and then.

Whatever happened, he stayed on much longer than he ever had before. He spent a lot of time sitting with the Queen and her ladies in the tower room. Sometimes I was with them, sometimes not. Sometimes I hated George Douglas for taking my Queen from me. Then one day they called me in.

George bolted the door behind me and they made me promise never to repeat to anyone what they were going to tell me. They had arranged between them how she would escape from the castle, but they couldn't do it without my help. Of course I promised to keep their secret and do what I could, and the Queen in turn promised that if she escaped she would take me with her. The castle would be no place for me to stay anyway after I had helped her to escape. They explained their plan to me. It was good, but it meant that we had to wait for the long weeks to pass until the first of May.

May is the beginning of summer – something special to celebrate after a long Scottish winter. In the castle they had the usual celebrations that we always used to have on the farm. The Queen and her ladies elected me as the 'Abbot of Unreason' for the day. That meant I had the right to go around playing jokes on anyone, and of course there was nothing they could do about it. The 'Abbot of Unreason' is king for the day. Even the soldiers joined in. Well, anything was a change from the long boring months of guarding that bleak, damp place. They enjoyed themselves, and by mid-morning most of them were laughing and joking and fairly drunk. We had arranged that once they were off guard I would slip

out and knock holes in all the boats on the island. All but one, that is. We had to keep that for the escape.

Sir William never approved of these celebrations, and he began to wonder what was going on, but the Queen managed to keep him busy enough inside the castle, so he never found out what I was doing. We were all set to go ahead with the plan, there was only one thing wanting and that was a message from George Douglas to say that he was ready with men and horses.

The message came just as they sat down to dinner. A man came over with a pair of earrings for the Queen. She told Sir William that she had lost them some time before, and that the man had found them for her. She had actually given them to George, and he had sent them back as a signal that all was ready, and he was waiting.

Dinner that night seemed to go on for ever. They were still celebrating of course, becoming more and more drunk. Even Sir William joined in the fun at last, so it was not difficult to steal the keys of the castle from him.

I crept down to the courtyard as fast and as quietly as I could. But I needn't have bothered being quiet, there were guards lying snoring on the stairs by then, and the noise could have been heard across the loch.

Queen Mary and her ladies were waiting for me in the dark shadows by the castle gates. Together we pulled open the heavy door. There was no guard to stop or challenge us, and she stepped out to freedom.

We locked the gates behind us, climbed into the one safe boat, and I pulled the oars with all the strength I had to take us away from that dreary place. Halfway across the loch we threw the keys into the water. Sir William was going to have some trouble getting out of his own castle! The Queen laughed at that and clapped her hands in delight.

George Douglas was waiting for us just as he had promised, in the shadow of the trees by the bank. He had stolen some of Sir William's best horses, so we made good speed and were well away before anyone realised what had happened.

We have ridden all night, and have only stopped for a rest at a house that belongs to a friend of George's. We will eat and drink, take fresh horses and leave ours here. Then we will ride on.

The Queen says that we must go to England, where she believes she has friends who will help her. I don't know what will happen now, but I do know that I will stay with my Queen as long as I live, and as long as she needs me.

Mary Queen of Scots

Queen Mary had escaped from Loch Leven Castle, but her
troubles were not over. She spent the first night at Niddry
Castle. Where should she go next? She could go to France,
where she had friends and supporters, or to England, where her
cousin, Queen Elizabeth, might help her. What would you have
done?

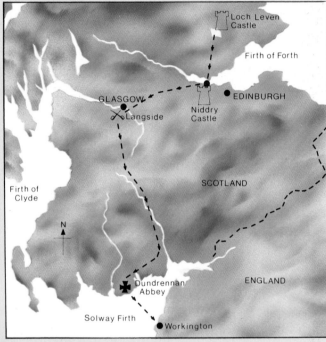

Before she had a
chance to decide, she
was forced to fight
her Scottish enemies
at Langside, near
Glasgow. The battle
was going very badly
for Mary's army, and
she fled south to
Dundrennan Abbey.

*Queen Mary's route
to England – nearly
150 km on horseback
without stopping for
food or drink.*

*Dundrennan Abbey,
the last place in
Scotland that
Mary ever saw.*

Mary Queen of Scots

Queen Elizabeth I of England

No-one really knows why Mary chose to go to England instead of to safety in France, but her trust in Elizabeth proved fatal. The English Queen was afraid that Mary would try to take the throne from her, so Mary was kept a prisoner for nineteen years. In all this time the cousins never met. Then a plot was discovered to kill Elizabeth and make Mary Queen of England. Mary was tried for high treason and beheaded on 8 February 1587.

The execution of Mary Queen of Scots at Fotheringhay Castle. Why do you think her clothes are being burnt outside?

Charlie's Bike

If you had asked Charlie what he wanted most in the world he would have given it some thought. He used to lie in bed at night, after all the lights went out, thinking about the things he wanted most.

He was going to drive a Formula One racing car one day. If he closed his eyes he could feel what it was like to take the bends at a hundred miles an hour. He could see the track tearing past him, and the black and white winner's flag at the end.

If he couldn't do that he was going to work on an oil rig like his big brother Pete, flying out by helicopter across the stormy North Sea, and coming home every few weeks with pockets full of money.

But these were things that would all have to wait a few years. If Charlie was sensible about it, the thing that he wanted most of all at the moment was a new bike.

Billy Anderson had had one for two months. And didn't everyone know about it? Even Johnnie Bee, who was always Charlie's best friend at school, deserted him sometimes to walk home with Billy and the new bike. Not that he got the chance to ride it though, but sometimes, just sometimes, Billy allowed him to push the bike. It gave Johnnie a great feeling walking along as if he owned it, but Billy always made loud remarks about it.

"Watch what you're doing with *my* bike will you," he would say, if they were passing someone on the pavement. "I don't want the paint scratched." So there was never any doubt about who that bike belonged to.

Charlie sniffed at this. "Just like him," he said to Johnnie. "Who wants a flashy bike like that anyway?"

But secretly he did. He looked at bikes in shop windows. He looked at them in the street. He spent hours looking at the photographs in his Mum's shopping catalogue.

"It's no use doing that," said Mum. "They're too expensive. Either you have a new bike or we eat for the next year. But not both."

"Och, Mum!" said Charlie. He knew she was kidding of course, but she still shook her head all the same.

Dad thought a new bike was a good idea. He liked the ones in the catalogue. He and Charlie spent a long time looking at them.

"Wait till I win the football pools, Charlie," he said. "Some day it'll happen." But somehow it never did.

And then one day something else happened. Pete came home from the oil rig. They always knew when he was coming because he sent a postcard to tell them. It was never a postcard like everyone else sent, with a picture of a place on it. It was always a joke one. Charlie collected them and stuck them up on the wall above his bed.

The latest postcard was very mysterious. 'Tell Charlie to stand by,' it said. 'Surprise coming.'

Charlie nearly wore out a track in the carpet that morning walking back and forward to the front window, looking down into the street for the taxi. He could see it coming from the corner, and by the time it pulled up at the front door he was down the three flights of stairs and across the grass to meet it.

A suitcase tumbled out, followed by Pete and then – wonder of wonders – a brand new bike.

It was beautiful. Gorgeous. Really the most

magnificent bike Charlie had ever seen. The frame
was blue and silver, there was a five-speed gear, and
low slung handlebars. A real racing bike. Charlie
stroked the saddle with his fingertips.

"One in the eye for Billy boy, eh?" laughed Pete.
He winked, ruffled Charlie's hair, grabbed his
suitcase and turned to wave to Mum who was
watching them from the window.

"Kettle on, Ma?" he called. "I'm coming up, and
I'm dying for a cup of tea."

Charlie pedalled off round the block. Slowly, so
that everyone would have a chance to see his new
bike, and wobbling a bit because the bike was rather
big for him.

"You take care now!" shouted Pete. Charlie
nodded his head and pedalled on.

Charlie loved that bike. He kept it upstairs in the hall, dragging it up and down three flights of stairs every time he wanted to use it, which was most of the time. If Mum asked him to go up to the corner shop for a loaf after school, he carried the bike down and cycled there. It would have been quicker to walk but not half so much fun. Johnnie Bee walked along with him and sometimes Charlie let him ride the bike back. It gave him a chance to stand back and see how good the bike looked on the road.

And then one day the awful thing happened. The bottom fell right out of Charlie's world.

The corner shop was busy because the factory across the road had just come out. There were big men in dark overalls pushing and shoving and joking with each other, all crowding in to buy cigarettes and newspapers. Charlie leaned the bike against the window and went inside. He had to wait a long time for his loaf.

At last it was his turn. He put the bread in a plastic bag, pushed back out into the street, and stopped dead in his tracks. The bike had gone!

He looked round. Maybe someone had moved it. But it was nowhere to be seen. Charlie rushed back into the shop.

Mr Patel shook his head sadly. "So many people,"

he said. "Someone must have taken it. Did you have a padlock on it?"

Charlie did have a padlock and key that Pete had given him with the bike. "I didn't think I needed to use it just outside the shop," he said.

Again Mr Patel shook his head. "You never know," he said.

Charlie ran home, swallowing hard to stop himself from crying. Hoping against hope that he wouldn't meet Johnnie or Billy Anderson. Not today of all days.

He made it back alone, fell in at the door and blurted out the story to Mum. They told Dad as soon as he came home from work. He sighed and pulled on his jacket again.

"We'll have to tell the police," he said. "Come on."

Charlie had never been inside the police station before. He had passed it often enough, but this was the first time he had ever been through the big glass doors. They stood in a waiting room with a black and white tile floor, waiting for someone to come to the desk and talk to them. Charlie looked around. The walls were covered in posters reminding people to lock up their cars, or their houses or their bikes. Charlie swallowed hard again.

The police sergeant looked at them over the counter and took out a notebook. "What was the number of the bike?" he asked.

"Number?" Charlie and Dad looked at each other.

"Every bike has a number," said the policeman. "Somewhere on the frame. If you can find out what it is we might be able to trace it for you."

"We never thought of that," said Dad, "but maybe Pete will know."

They phoned Pete that night. At least Mum did. Charlie didn't really feel like talking to him. He could hear Pete explode at the other end of the line, but at last he calmed down.

"He's got it," said Mum. "He made a note of it on the card they gave him in the shop. He's just gone to find it."

Charlie sighed with relief.

"That doesn't mean you'll get it back though," said Mum. "The police still have to find it."

Weeks passed and nothing happened. Charlie hated going to the shop. He went the long way round over the back wall and along the lane so that he wouldn't have to meet Billy Anderson. He sat on the edge of the pavement with Johnnie throwing stones in the gutter.

"Rotten it is, just rotten," he said.

"Maybe it's been pinched by a gang of international jewel thieves and they're using it for a robbery!" said Johnnie hopefully.

"Don't talk daft," said Charlie. Sometimes he thought Johnnie was just a bit stupid.

Then one day, as Charlie trailed his schoolbag up the road, he saw Mum leaning out of the window and waving to him. "Hurry up," she called. "Come on, quick!"

Charlie threw the bag over his shoulder and ran up the stairs two at a time.

"The police think they've found your bike," said Mum. "They've arrested some man who broke into a house and his garage is full of all sorts of things. You'll have to go down to the station and identify it."

When Charlie got to the police station the sergeant took him through a door to a room at the back. There were tables with radios, watches, a fur coat, some jewellery and several other bits and pieces.

And leaning against the wall there was a bike. It wasn't a blue and silver bike. It was red, but it did have a five-speed gear and dropped handlebars.

"That's not mine," said Charlie. "My bike isn't red."

"It's been repainted," said the policeman. "They often do that when they pinch things. The number's on the frame though. Here, try it."

Charlie climbed on to the bike and bounced up and down on the saddle. "I think it's mine," he said. "But it's got smaller."

The policeman laughed. "No it hasn't," he said. "It's just that you've grown bigger waiting for it. It fits you fine now."

"Can I take it home?" said Charlie.

"I'm afraid not," said the policeman. "We have to keep your bike for a while anyway. It's important evidence. If we can identify where it came from we can put the thief behind bars for a while. You'll get it back after the trial."

Charlie sat on the edge of the pavement that night with Johnnie Bee. They were chucking stones in the gutter.

"He'll get years in jail," said Charlie. "You should have seen the stuff he'd pinched. Radios and jewels and all that!"

"Well!" said Johnnie. His eyes were huge and round just thinking about it. Then he said, "You see, I was right. It *was* a sort of gang of international jewel thieves after all."

"Well, there was only one, and I wouldn't really call it international. Not down our road!" said Charlie, laughing. But he was too happy to be bothered arguing about it.

Calum and the Promise of Gold

There was once a young man called Calum who lived in a small cottage by himself. The cottage was old and tumbledown. The one field that went with it had very poor soil, full of weeds and stones. Instead of working to mend his cottage and to dig the stones and weeds from his field, Calum grumbled all day long about how hard his life was. It was unfair, he said, that some people had fine houses, good land and gold to spend, while he had none.

He was grumbling in this way to a neighbour one day. The neighbour laughed and shook his head.

"Aye Calum," he said, "I have good land, I'll grant you, but only because I worked long and hard to make it so."

Calum wouldn't listen. Nothing would please him but to believe that the world was unfair to him. He soon became known among his neighbours as Calum the Grumbler and fewer and fewer people came to see him. Did that stop his grumbling? No, of course not.

It happened one day that he was working in his field. As he dug he grumbled to himself, and at last he stood up and threw down his spade.

"It's no use," he said. "No use at all! There are far too many stones."

He sat down on a rock for a rest. He sat for a long
time, until the sun slowly sank behind the high hills
at the head of the glen, and the birds, wheeling and
dancing against the evening sky, returned to their
nests. At last, just as the sun vanished, he sighed and
stretched.

"I wish I could have gold," he said. "Enough to
fill this field and my wee cottage as well. Then I'd be
happy."

"Would your name be Calum then?" came a voice
from behind him.

Calum spun round to find a little man in a long green cloak, such as travellers wore at that time, and a wide-brimmed hat that almost hid his face.

"Is your name Calum?" repeated the little man. "Calum the Grumbler they call you in the village."

"What if it is?" said Calum rudely. "And who might you be?"

"Ah well," said the little man, "let's just say that I'm the guardian of that stone you were sitting on. You sat there and made a wish, and I'm in a position to do something about it. I can cover your field with gold, fill up your wee house as well, and make you the happiest man in the world."

"How can you help?" asked Calum, laughing. "A poor wee thing like you? Can you turn this rock I'm sitting on to gold just now?"

"No – no, I can't do that," said the little man.

"Well, maybe you can change these old clothes of mine into fine new clothes with gold buttons and lace trimmings, like the gentry wear. Come on, let's see you do that."

"No," said the little man. "I can't do that either. Not just now."

"Then what is it you can do?" asked Calum. "What I want is gold, enough to fill my field and my house. That will bring me happiness."

"Well," said the little man, looking at him thoughtfully, "there's gold and gold. But there's only one sort of happiness. I tell you what, Calum the Grumbler, you do as I say for a year and a day, and we shall see what we shall see."

"What must I do then?" asked Calum.

"You must work," said the little man. "You must work from the hour the sun comes over the hills, until it sets over the blue islands of the western sea. You must clear this field of stones, and with the stones you must build a wall round the field, as high as a man's waist."

"That's hard work!" protested Calum.

"And then," said the little man, ignoring him, "you must help your neighbours in their fields. In return they will give you a bag of corn seeds that you will plant here, and while they are growing you will keep the field clear of weeds and protect the corn from birds and beasts."

"And if I do?" demanded Calum.

"If you do that, I will come back at the end of a year and a day," said the little man.

"And give me my gold?" asked Calum.

"You will have your gold," laughed the little man.

"Enough to fill the field and my house as well?"

"Enough and more," said the little man. Then he

turned, walked off down the field, and vanished into the gathering darkness.

The next morning Calum was up early. He worked hard from morning until night, digging the thick brown earth. He filled basket after basket with stones, and as each basket was full he dragged it to the edge of the field to build the wall. It was hard work, and as the sun set over the blue islands, Calum was glad to go home to his cottage. But a cold cottage it was, with no light in the windows, and no fire in the hearth. Calum ate a lonely meal of bread and cheese and fell asleep.

Every morning after that he was out working in his field by the time the sun rose over the hills. There were days when the work was so hard that he felt like giving up, but then he remembered what the little man had promised.

"I will have gold to myself," said Calum. "And there will be no happier man in all the world."

He set to work digging faster than ever. The neighbours passing by on the road stopped and stared to see Calum the Grumbler working so hard.

"He'll make a fine job of that field," they said. "If he keeps working like that he'll be a good farmer yet."

At last Calum's field was cleared of stones and the wall around it was as high as a man's waist. Calum then went to his neighbours and offered to work for them, and as the little man had said, they gave him a sack of corn seeds in return.

He had worked so well that they all came to help him plant his corn. Because the farmers came, their wives came too. And as farmers' wives will, they set to work in Calum's cottage. They swept, polished, dusted and mended, all the time chattering like sparrows in the springtime.

Calum was amazed when he came home to his cottage that night. "My," he said, "it's so clean and bright. I think I must find myself a wife as well."

The farmers' wives nodded their heads, saying it was about time that he was married. The farmers' daughters threw their aprons over their heads and giggled. The one who giggled loudest was a pretty, plump dark-eyed girl from the village, called Bessie. Calum laughed and tickled her, and Bessie giggled more than ever.

She and Calum became friends. It was not long before he was calling for Bessie after church every Sunday to go out walking. Calum wore his best blue cap, and Bessie wore her mother's good red shawl with the golden fringes. Everyone agreed they made a very fine picture.

And so the year turned. Calum worked hard in his field, clearing the ground of weeds when the first green shoots of corn began to grow in the spring.

There were places where the wall round the field was not so high. Calum dug more stones from the little garden round the cottage to fill in the spaces, and having dug the garden over, he planted it with potatoes and cabbages and turnips. He worked long and hard, and after a while he had almost forgotten about the little man and his promise. Just sometimes, as he was working, he would stop and stretch his back and smile.

"Ah, the gold I will have," he thought to himself. "There will be no happier man in all the world."

In the summer-time when the corn was still green, Calum and Bessie were married. She came to live with him in the cottage and brought her grandmother's old copper kettle and the red shawl with the golden fringes.

She spread the shawl over the bed and in the little dark room the golden fringes shone bright, like a field of buttercups. Her grandmother's kettle sat by the fire. Because it was so old and had been polished every single day for a hundred years, it shone like the sun and filled the little kitchen with light. And so Calum and Bessie lived very happily.

The long warm summer days turned at last to autumn. The mornings were fresh and misty, and Calum began again to think about the little man. Exactly a year had passed since the day when he had last spoken to him in the field.

The next morning Calum rose early, before Bessie was awake, dressed and went out. He stood at the cottage door, looking down across his field of corn, still and grey in the early-morning mist.

"Aye," said a voice at his side. "You're up and about early, my man."

Calum turned, and there stood the little man. "I am that," said Calum. "I've done as you told me, and now I have come to look for my gold. You promised you would cover my field, fill my cottage with it and make me the happiest man in the world. So where is it?"

The little man laughed. "Look around you," he said. "Look around. I told you, there's gold, and there's gold."

As Calum watched, the early morning sun rose above the high hills, and the soft grey mist melted as though it had never been. As the first rays of sunlight touched the field, it turned to a thick quilt of rich

golden corn. Behind him in the cottage Bessie sang
quietly as she went about her work at the start of a
new day. Calum turned and watched her. In the
hearth the fire burned bright and welcoming, and the
flames sparkled like gold on the little copper kettle
that had been polished every day for a hundred years.

"It's a fine morning!" called Bessie, as she threw
open the windows, filling the cottage with the golden
September sunlight.

Calum turned to the little man, but he had
vanished like the mist. He threw back his head and
laughed. "It is indeed a fine morning," he shouted.
"And I am the happiest man in all the world."

Manhunt

The trail of footprints led up across the snow, away
from the beach. The left foot showed the print of a
heavy rubber sea boot. The right one was a bare foot.
Here and there a patch of blood stained the blinding
white snow.

Shouts and a shot rang out from the beach.
Soldiers in grey uniforms started to climb, stumbling
and slipping in the snow.

Further up, a young man lay gasping for breath
behind a boulder. He could hear his heart pounding
with fear. The shouts of soldiers echoed across the
still, sunlit waters around the island. On the stones of
the beach below lay the men who had come with him
on this mission. Ten minutes before, they had been
asleep in a fishing boat. Now that boat was sunk and
the others were prisoners or dead. Jan alone was free,
but it could not be for much longer.

He shivered in his wet clothes. His right foot was
bleeding where a bullet had hit him. He must have
lost the sea boot when he jumped into the water. Jan
knew only too well the dangers of frostbite. He
started to rub the frozen white skin of his foot.

A shout from below stopped him. Four men had
found his tracks and were climbing towards him. He

knew there was nowhere else to hide. As soon as he left the shelter of the gully and ran they would surely shoot him down.

He watched them come, pulling out his gun. He knew they would try to take him alive. They had to make him tell the names of the men he had come to meet. Jan lifted his pistol in hands that were shaking with cold. He waited until the officer in front came closer.

His finger tightened on the trigger. He stared into the other man's eyes and fired. Nothing happened!

The gun he had carried ashore from the boat was frozen. Blocked with ice! He shook it and hit it against the hard ground. Just as the officer reached out to grab him Jan fired again, and the man fell at his feet. The soldiers coming up behind paused for a second. Jan turned and fired, hitting the nearest man. The others ran for cover.

It was all the start he needed. Hardly stopping to look back he stumbled up the hill away from the gully. In the snow his dark jacket made him a clear target. Among the rocks of the hill-top he would be safer.

He climbed over the top and down to the beach on the other side of the island. Behind him he could hear the search parties. He could see two wooden sheds where farmers stored hay for the winter months. Jan longed to climb into the hay, take off his wet clothes and sleep. He knew it was useless. The huts were the first place the soldiers would look. He had to leave the island, but there was no boat.

There was no other way out. He must swim to safety. Across the narrow channel there lay another island. It was smaller, but closer to the mainland. Jan took a deep breath and walked out into the icy water. It was the beginning of the greatest and most dangerous adventure of his life.

It had all started for Jan Baalsrud some years before.
He was a Norwegian, who lived in the city of Oslo
with his father and sister. When the Second World
War broke out he had joined the army. When the
Germans invaded and occupied Norway in 1940, Jan
fled over the border to Sweden. At that time Sweden
was a neutral country and took no part in the war.
From there he and his friends carried on the fight.
He travelled between Sweden and Norway, bringing
back information that could be passed on to the
British. He also helped other Norwegians to escape
through Sweden to safety.

The time came when he was warned that the Germans knew what he was doing. Jan had to leave Sweden and come to England. He was standing in Piccadilly Circus in the heart of London, wondering what he should do next, when a British officer came up to him. They had known each other in Sweden. He suggested that Jan should join a group who were being trained in Scotland to go back to Norway and fight the Germans.

"But how do I get into Norway?" asked Jan.

"The Shetland Bus," was the answer. And that was how Jan came to be on the fishing boat.

Shetland fishing boats in the 1940s

The Shetland Islands are the most northerly part of Britain. Many Norwegians who had been fishermen before the war knew them well. When war broke out they escaped from the Germans simply by crossing the North Sea in fishing boats to Shetland. This gave them the idea to continue using the little boats which could come and go easily.

A base was set up by the British Navy in Shetland. Working with the fishermen, they converted the boats to carry explosives. Guns were hidden in oil drums on the decks. The Norwegian crews wore no uniforms. All the clothes they had were bought in Norway. In that way, if they were caught they would appear to be simply local fishermen.

The Shetland Buses only sailed during the winter months when the short days and long dark nights gave them more cover. The weather was dangerous and conditions hard, but the men knew the coast and islands of Norway well. Winter after winter they went on taking arms to the men and women of Norway to help them in their fight. Sometimes they brought out people for whom the Germans were hunting. Sometimes they took in agents who had been trained to blow up railway lines, airfields and fuel dumps. These agents would be landed on some small island off the coast and passed from one safe house to another until they reached their target. With luck they could escape by catching another 'Bus' back to Shetland.

Jan Baalsrud and three friends had been trained as agents in Scotland. They had spent a year living in the mountains, learning how to fight, how to handle explosives, and how to survive in the hard winter weather. Jan sailed for Norway full of hope that he would be able to help in the fight to free his country.

But before that fight began the Germans were warned. A warship was sent to sink the fishing boat and capture the men aboard. Jan was the only one of the twelve agents and crew to escape.

His story after he left the island is an exciting and terrifying one. He spent many months hiding from the Germans. Everywhere he went people helped him. He was given dry clothes and skis. But he had to walk for miles, sleeping often in the open, suffering from the frostbite he had feared so much.

On one occasion he came through a village early in the morning. As he passed the schoolhouse the doors suddenly opened and dozens of German soldiers poured out. Unknown to Jan they had been using the school as a base. Unable to turn back, he went down the road, through the soldiers. Not one of them seemed to notice the small dark man in the naval

jacket with the word NORWAY written in English on the shoulder. It was an amazing piece of luck.

He wandered on across the barren mountains of Norway. Often his worst enemy was not the Germans but the weather. It might have killed another man but Jan had a great deal of courage. He suffered terribly from the cold. His feet became so bad that in the end he had to cut off some of his toes. If he had not done this he would probably have lost his legs from frostbite.

Somehow he survived. Eventually he was brought to the Swedish border by a group of wandering Lapp people. He lay on the sledge on which they had dragged him for miles across snow and ice, and listened to the strange voices around him. And then came a word he knew. They were talking of a lake. Jan knew it was the lake which formed part of the border between Norway and Sweden. Pulling himself up, he looked around – and there below them lay the lake. The ice was frozen, glittering in the sun. It was the road to freedom!

Jan begged the Lapps to take him across. They shook their heads. They lifted handfuls of snow and let it fall, dripping. He knew that they were trying to tell him that the ice was melting. They were afraid to cross. He could see patches of green where the ice was thinner. He begged them to cross quickly, but some still shook their heads.

As they stood arguing, a shot rang out. A party of soldiers was coming over the hill towards them. They had found Jan at last.

"Run!" he screamed. "Move!"

He pulled out the gun he had carried all the way from the boat. It was useless now, frozen solid and rusted, but he waved it. As soon as the Lapps saw the gun they began to run, pulling his sledge with them.

Jan never knew whether they were afraid of the soldiers or not. Perhaps they thought that he would shoot them. They rushed down the hill towards the frozen lake in a mass. They dashed out across the ice away from the soldiers. Bullets skidded off the ice. Around them the surface creaked and groaned. Somehow Jan's amazing luck held. The ice did not break.

At last they reached the other side and clambered up the beach on to Swedish soil. Jan knew that the hunt was over and he had reached freedom at last.